TRUST ME, HANSEL AND GRETEL ARE *SWEET!*

The story of **HANSEL AND GRETEL**

as told by
THE WITCH

by **Nancy Loewen**

illustrated by **Janna Bock**

raintree

a Capstone company — publishers for children

Raintree is an imprint of Capstone Global Library Limited, a company incorporated in England and Wales having its registered office at 7 Pilgrim Street, London, EC4V 6LB – Registered company number: 6695582

www.raintree.co.uk
myorders@raintree.co.uk

Editor: Jill Kalz
Designer: Ted Williams
Creative Director: Nathan Gassman
Production Specialist: Jennifer Walker
The illustrations in this book were created digitally.
Printed and bound in China.

ISBN 978 1 4747 1014 5
20 19 18 17 16
10 9 8 7 6 5 4 3 2 1

British Library Cataloguing in Publication Data
A full catalogue record for this book is available from the British Library.

Special thanks to our adviser, Terry Flaherty, PhD, Professor of English, Minnesota State University, Mankato, USA, for his expertise.

Yes, I'm the witch from the Hansel and Gretel story. And yes, I live in a house made of gingerbread.

But I most certainly did NOT tumble into the flames of my own oven. (I mean, look at me – I'm alive!) And NEVER would I think of EATING Hansel and Gretel.

It's time I set the record straight. Gather around. (But please, no nibbling on the house.)

I always knew I was different. While the other little
witches were learning to make potions and cast spells,
I was playing with my food. I shaped mashed potato
into polar bears. I wove spaghetti into wall hangings.

As I grew up, my projects got bigger and better. I was a food artist!
I made beds out of marshmallows and floors out of liquorice.
Eventually I built my own cottage. **My masterpiece.**

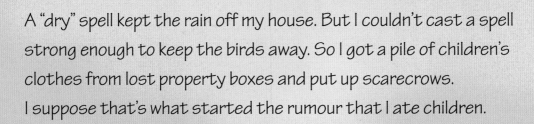

A "dry" spell kept the rain off my house. But I couldn't cast a spell strong enough to keep the birds away. So I got a pile of children's clothes from lost property boxes and put up scarecrows. I suppose that's what started the rumour that I ate children.

The scarecrows did the trick – except for one crow who wasn't the least bit scared. I called him Thorn. Every day I had to patch up the holes he made. It was an ongoing battle.

Not long ago I was out back doing touch-up work when I heard
children's voices. A shutter snapped. A window shattered.

Little hooligans were eating my house!

I ran around to the front. "Stop that this instant!"
I shouted. "This is private property!"

The children, a boy and a girl, stared at me in horror.

"We're sorry!" said the girl. "But we're so hungry!"

"Please don't eat us!" the boy begged.

I could see that the children didn't look well. So I invited them in for something to eat. Their names were Hansel and Gretel. Between bites they told me quite a story.

"Our stepmother wanted to get rid of us," Gretel said. "She said there wasn't enough food for us, but she just wanted it all for herself."

"She made Dad leave us in the forest – twice! She was hoping we'd get lost," said Hansel. "The first time we made a trail with white pebbles and followed it back home."

"The second time we made a trail with bread crumbs," Gretel continued. "But—"

"Let me guess," I said. "The birds ate the crumbs?"

The children nodded.

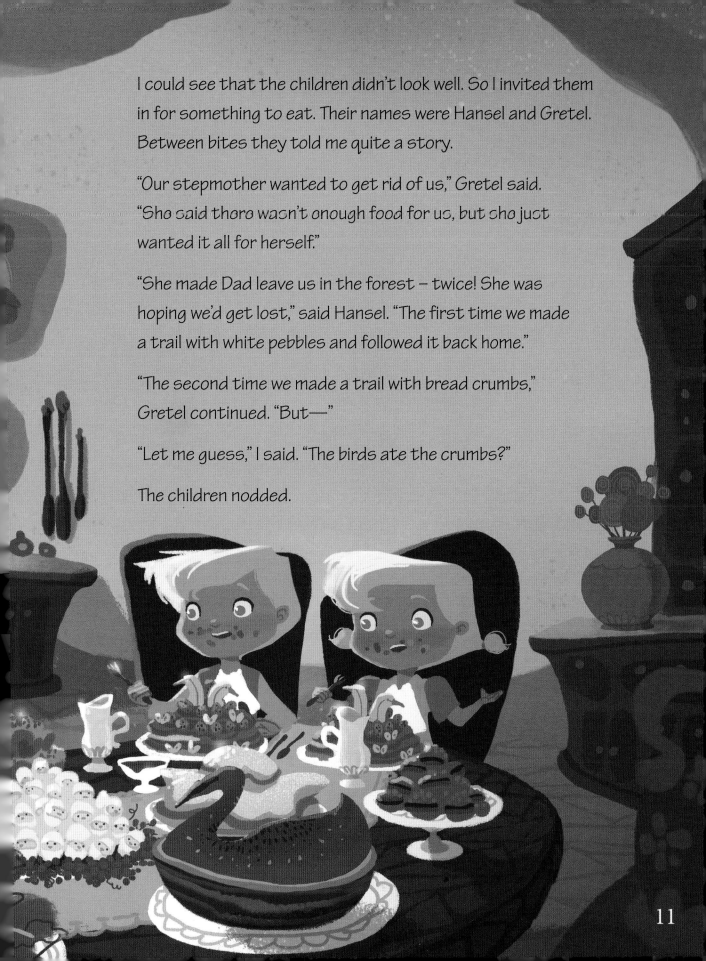

Of course I said they could live with me.
Where else would they go?

Hansel, Gretel and I got on beautifully. I taught
them about food art. They helped me with my
housework and kept an eye on that horrible bird.

13

Hansel was a natural artist. He made a wonderful sculpture of himself out of sponge cake and dried fruit. Sometimes I teased him by talking to it. "Oh, Hansel, I want to gobble you up!" I'd say.

Life was sweet.

I didn't even have to worry about Thorn anymore. One day he just disappeared.

But, you know, it was too good to be true. A bird like that never gives up.

A few weeks later, the children and I were baking pies. Suddenly Thorn landed on my window and began pecking away. Then a woman's voice called,

"Yoo-hoo! Is anyone home?"

Hansel and Gretel turned as white as icing sugar. Their wicked stepmother!

Yes, the stepmother and Thorn were working together! They wanted the children and me out of the picture so they could eat my house. Well, THAT wasn't going to happen.

I flung open the door. "Now look here," I began, but the woman pushed past me.

"Darling children, you're alive!" she exclaimed.

"Run for it!" I told Hansel and Gretel.

I grabbed a pie and was about to throw it in the stepmother's face - when she opened the oven door and shoved me in!

(I know this is a very scary part of the story. If you need to take a few deep breaths, that's fine.)

19

So there I was, shouting and pounding on the oven door. But then I realized something: The flames weren't burning me. In fact they tickled.

My dear old oven, my true and best friend, would NEVER harm me.

When the stepmother checked to see if I was burnt to a crisp, out I popped. Not a toasted hair on my head!

She ran away, shrieking. Thorn flew close behind. They were never heard from again.

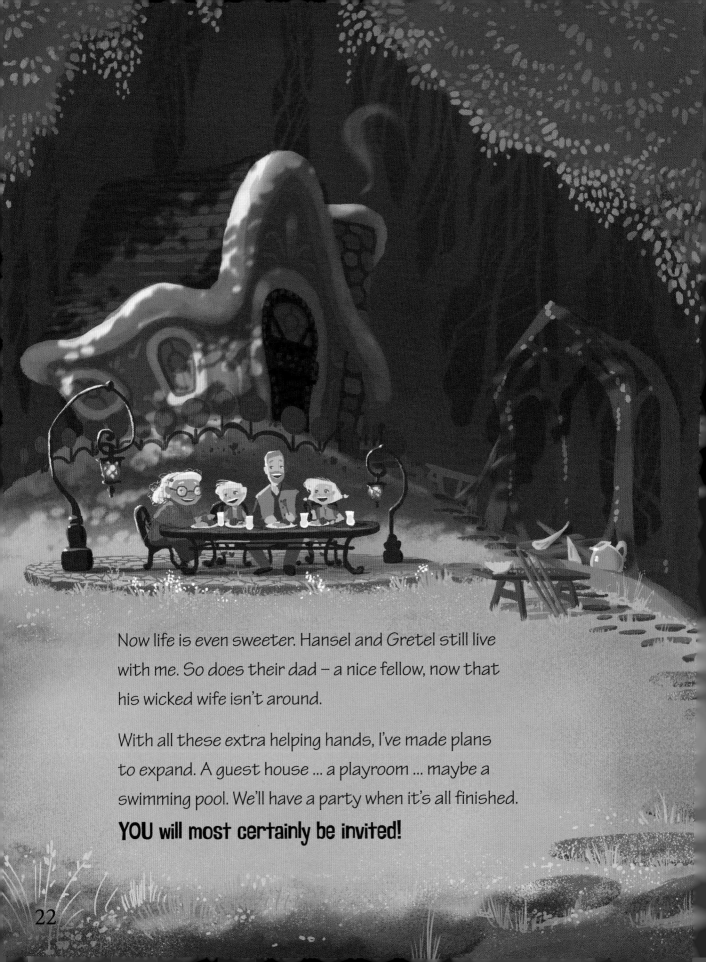

Now life is even sweeter. Hansel and Gretel still live with me. So does their dad – a nice fellow, now that his wicked wife isn't around.

With all these extra helping hands, I've made plans to expand. A guest house ... a playroom ... maybe a swimming pool. We'll have a party when it's all finished. **YOU will most certainly be invited!**

Discussion points

Look in your local library or online to find the original "Hansel and Gretel" story. Describe how the character of the witch looks and acts. Compare and contrast her with the witch in this version of the story.

Rain and hungry visitors mean trouble for the witch's gingerbread house. Explain how the witch tries to keep her cottage safe. Which methods work? Which methods don't work?

If Thorn told the story instead of the witch, what details might he tell differently? What if Hansel told the story? How might his point of view differ?

Thorn is a character who doesn't speak, and yet his actions are an important part of the plot. What do the illustrations tell you about Thorn?

Glossary

character person, animal or creature in a story
plot what happens in a story
point of view way of looking at something
version account of something from a certain
    point of view

Read more

Fairy Tales (Writing Stories), Anita Ganeri (Raintree, 2014)

Pandarella (Animal Fairy Tales), Charlotte Guillain (Raintree, 2013)

The Unhappy Stonecutter (Folk Tales From Around the World), Charlotte Guillain (Raintree, 2014)

Website

www.bbc.co.uk/programmes/p02tc9c2

Abandoned by their parents, Hansel and Gretel met a witch who wanted to eat them. After Gretel pushed her into the fire, they lived happily ever after - or so the story goes.

Look out for all the books in this series:

Believe Me, Goldilocks Rocks!
Believe Me, I Never Felt a Pea!
Frankly, I'd Rather Spin Myself a New Name!
Frankly, I Never Wanted to Kiss Anybody!
Honestly, Red Riding Hood Was Rotten!
No Kidding, Mermaids Are a Joke!
No Lie, I Acted Like a Beast!

No Lie, Pigs (and Their Houses) CAN Fly!
Really, Rapunzel Needed a Haircut!
Seriously, Cinderella Is SO Annoying!
Seriously, Snow White Was SO Forgetful!
Truly, We Both Loved Beauty Dearly!
Trust Me, Hansel and Gretel Are SWEET!
Trust Me, Jack's Beanstalk Stinks!